HIS VIRGIN NANNY

THE VIRGIN PACT - BOOK 2

JESSA JAMES

His Virgin Nanny: Copyright © 2017 by Jessa James

ISBN: 978-1-7959-0196-3

All Rights Reserved. No part of this book may be reproduced or transmitted in any form or by any means, electrical, digital or mechanical including but not limited to photocopying, recording, scanning or by any type of data storage and retrieval system without express, written permission from the author.

Published by Jessa James
James, Jessa
His Virgin Nanny

Cover design copyright 2017 by Jessa James, Author
Images/Photo Credit: Stocksy: Julien L. Balmer

Publisher's Note:

This book was written for an adult audience. The book may contain explicit sexual content. Sexual activities included in this book are strictly fantasies intended for adults and any activities or risks taken by fictional characters within the story are neither endorsed nor encouraged by the author or publisher.

1

abe

I HADN'T EVEN MADE IT THROUGH THE FRONT DOOR OF my best friend's house and my dick was hard. It wasn't because of him. It wasn't just Greg who'd answered the door, but with him were two young women. One was his new love interest, Jane. And although she was pretty, it was her friend who made me feel like a little kid who'd just seen tits for the first time. Not only did she get my attention, but my dick's, too.

When Greg told me he had someone in mind to babysit my niece, I was expecting some socially awkward teenager who'd gotten the short end of the puberty stick. Wasn't that how babysitters were portrayed in movies, complete with the glasses, bangs, and forehead of pimples?

I looked at *her* – Mary – from head to toe. Yes, she had the bangs, but her emerald eyes were scot-free of any glasses, and every inch of her gorgeous skin looked flawless. It didn't even look like she was wearing makeup, it was so subtle, yet she could turn heads. It did mine.

I blinked my eyes a couple of times and instantly glanced at those D-cups. I hadn't meant to, but they were pointing right at me. When I brought my head up, I could see Mary's smirk curved very slightly into a small grin. I was good at reading people; Mary liked the way I was looking at her. The way I was reacting to just the sight of her. I should behave, I knew it, but I couldn't control the urge to ogle her. What I *really* wanted was to *touch,* kiss, taste that creamy skin, put a flush on her cheeks as I made her whimper with need, fill her with my dick and watch her curves bounce as I thrust hard and deep. God, I was screwed and I hadn't even gotten past the doorway.

I was an animal for thinking about her in such a way, but she was gorgeous, with her oval-shaped face and high cheekbones…and sexy, too, with slender legs, a full ass, and an endowed rack. Her hair was long and dark, almost black, framing her perfect face, pouting pink lips and green eyes that sparkled with innocence and desire at the same time. The look made my entire body go on high alert, my cock turning rock hard.

His Virgin Nanny

This was a woman I could teach, protect and thoroughly enjoy introducing to the world of sex and heat and breath-stealing pleasure. I had no doubt she was innocent. She might have fucked a high school boy before, but there was no doubt she'd never been with a man. With most women, I usually had to pick between innocent and sexy. I couldn't haven't both. But Mary? She was perfection. I wanted her.

Which was stupid. She was eighteen. Jane's best friend. The fucking babysitter. And just that fast, I felt like a schmuck. A real asshole. But this was insta-love or some shit like that because she was going to be mine. Mary was mine, she just didn't know it yet.

"Hey man, you alright?" Greg's words brought me back down to Earth.

"Yeah," I easily recovered from my daydreaming/salivating. "So, you're Mary?"

Our eyes maintained contact – my azure ones meeting her green ones. She looked at me with her bottom lip pouting slightly, and her arms were crossed, one over the other, to rest below her breasts. With the additional support, her cleavage deepened, and so did her smile. I didn't know which to look at.

"It's nice to meet you…"

"Gabe," came my smooth reply, as I extended my arm to shake her hand.

"That's so formal," Mary responded. She took a step, then two, closer to me, opening her arms wide and brought me into a hug. I was too surprised to hug her back, too caught up in the feel of her breasts pressing against my chest.

"Don't tell me you hug your teachers that way?" I asked, my tone teasing. When she pulled away, she raised an eyebrow at me and turned to face Greg. He taught Civics and Government at the nearby private school for girls, and Mary had been his student. She just graduated and wanted to earn some extra income before college started in the fall, and it just so happened I was looking for a sitter.

I'd promised my sister I'd look after Ashley, her two-year-old, during her six-month deployment to the Middle East, but I still needed to work. As an architect, construction sites weren't exactly the place to take a two-year-old. When I stole a glance at Mary, I couldn't help but think she was heaven-sent. Not only did she look like an angel, but she was one, too. I wouldn't know what I'd do without a sitter. I loved my niece, but I couldn't be with her twenty-four/seven. Besides, I had no mothering instincts whatsoever.

"Isn't anyone hungry yet? I'm starving!" Jane exclaimed. Greg had met his match with her, and by the satisfied look on his face, he'd put her in her place: beneath him. Or maybe on his lap. Or on her hands and knees. I wasn't interested in Jane, and my thoughts shifted to thinking about Mary in those positions. With me.

"Did Greg wear you out? Is that why you're hungry?" Mary teased her friend and I choked, shocked. Yeah, I'd had similar thoughts, but those words from sweet Mary?

I switched my glance from Jane to Greg repeatedly, and I could see Jane's cheeks start to turn red. That was the kind of shit I liked to give Greg non-stop, and that was exactly why we were friends. That Mary was joining in on the fun made her twice as interesting. I just hoped I could get *her* to blush like that.

I couldn't help but stare at the girl…or rather, woman. Woman – that was what I meant. For a couple of eighteen-year-olds, Mary and Jane looked mature, all grown-up – in an *extremely* good way. Their clothes were tight, hugging perky breasts and tight asses, but Mary knocked me dead with a megawatt smile that make my dick stir. Which was not good, not right now. Not on Greg's front stoop. But a man who didn't stare at them was probably gay. It was no wonder Greg was nuts for Jane, that he got some all the time.

When he first told me he had the hots for an eighteen-year-old, I gave him shit. Greg was handsome, and he knew how to work the beard. He was even a lawyer, or would be once he passed the Bar exam. He was a catch. Women his age would flaunt themselves at him, but according to him, there was just something about Jane, something that actually made him get into a committed relationship. Last time I talked to him, he was thinking marriage—which was nuts. He hadn't asked Jane yet, but she'd practically moved in with him. Her family was usually off traveling the world, so devoting her time to Greg appeared to be an easy choice. And if I had a woman like her in my bed every night...

"You're just jealous you don't have a hot, young girlfriend...and sex-on-demand," returned Greg. Yeah, he'd read my mind.

"That was gold, man." I clapped my friend on the back. "You got me there. No sex-on-demand, and I'm done with the one-night-stands."

"Hmmm..." My head moved to look at the owner of the soft voice. Mary was looking at me with a curious brow raised before she curved her lips up into a small smile. Then, she looked away and wrapped an arm around Jane's.

"I heard we're having steaks," she said. "I'll help get things ready."

"All the food's been prepped," Greg told her. "I just need to grill the steaks. Come on in."

Greg and Jane, hand in hand, led us toward the kitchen.

Mary said, "Thank you for inviting me over for dinner, Mr. Parker. Your home's lovely."

"No, thank *you*," came his response before he glanced at me for a second. "You'll be doing Gabe a huge favor by looking after his niece this summer."

"No problem, I *love* children," she replied, her tone almost cooing, as she met my eyes. "How often does she need to be watched?"

Before I could open my mouth to speak, Greg was

His Virgin Nanny

quick to say, "Before you two talk business and start being boring, let's eat first. Potatoes and salad are ready, and the steak will come in a few minutes."

With a series of nods, the three of us took our seats. I sat beside Mary, our legs touching beneath the table, and I couldn't help the sudden stirring feeling inside me.

Damn.

Damn. Damn. Damn. I was in trouble. My dick was getting a zipper imprint just because our thighs were touching.

That was all I thought throughout dinner. When Mary tied her ebony hair up into a ponytail, exposing her nape, I couldn't help but hitch my breath. I tried my best to be as subtle as possible. When Mary opened her luscious, red lips to take a bite of the steak, I used all my willpower not to wonder what they would look like around my dick. When she easily contributed to the conversation with her light, feminine voice, I discovered she was smart and witty as well as beautiful. Everything about her – I just wanted to experience more. *Hell*, I fucking wanted to taste her. All of her.

"How's your steak?" she asked.

Out of courtesy and a little nudge from my dick, I glanced at her, more like stared, actually. Her lips curved up into a small smile, and she turned so her upper torso leaned toward me. My eyes glanced down to look at her cleavage. I couldn't help it. I was only a man and fuck... it was lush and she was more than a handful. I clenched my fists so I wouldn't cup her in my palms and feel how heavy they were, see how they overflowed over my fingers. When I looked back up, her smile had turned into a curious smirk. It was as if she was taunting me.

There was no doubt she was flirting. I'd had experience with women trying to grab my attention; I knew most of what they stored in their bag of tricks, and it looked like Mary was playing the same game. I shook my head subtly. I didn't want to think about it too much. She was eighteen years old.

When I'd been eighteen, I was an awkward, lanky kid who didn't know how to flirt. The girls back then were the same. We were all naïve and knew close to nothing when it came to attracting the opposite sex. From the looks of it, Mary had no problem with getting *my* attention. Hell, I wasn't going to be able to forget her. No, her scent, her eyes, her curves were burned into my brain. She had me, and my dick, wrapped around her little finger.

"Gabe?" she called out my name when I still hadn't responded to her.

"It's great. Want a bite?"

Automatically, I sliced my meat, forked the small portion, and held it up right in front her mouth. I saw the way her eyes widened at my gesture, surprise painted on her face. Looking at her, I couldn't move my head away. From her high cheekbones and full lips, every part of her complemented each other to form a masterpiece. She finally leaned forward, opened her lips, and had a taste of my steak. When the medium-rare meat touched her tongue, she closed her eyes, savoring the taste, before she opened them again. Holy fuck, the sound she made. Part moan, part gasp, I wanted her to make that sound again, but when she came all over my cock.

This was an intro to a fucking porn video.

Especially with the way she looked and moved – feminine, youthful, and yet calculating – it was hard not to want to know more about her. She didn't act or speak or look like an eighteen-year-old. My dick didn't care about her age. She was legal, she was gorgeous, she was smart, she was into me. She was mine.

As dinner continued and conversation lengthened and turned lighter and more informal, I was starting to see her as someone who didn't let herself be dictated by her age. She talked about her plans for the future; she was going to take up early education since she wanted to be a pre-school teacher. It was noble, and I saw myself wanting to know everything about her. She wasn't just the gorgeous and sexy Catholic schoolgirl that made my dick hard, although the thought of her in her plaid uniform skirt was making my cock press painfully against the zipper of my jeans.

She was a complex human being who wanted more in life than just to coast through. She had hopes and dreams and was going to move across the country for college.

"Are you ready for the big move yet?" I asked her. Jane had just come back from the kitchen to take the strawberry cheesecake from the refrigerator. She cut a slice each for us, handed the plates over, then took her seat beside Greg. All eyes turned to Mary.

"Hmm..." There was a tinge of hesitation in her voice. "Not really. Honestly, I don't want to move, and I planned to go to the local college, but my mom keeps telling me that specific college is the best for a degree in education. And that's the only school she'll pay for."

I frowned. "I'm sure you can talk to her about it," I offered, tilting my lips up into a warm smile which she returned. Her mom sounded like a bitch if she was dictating where her daughter went to school. Withholding money for any other place? That was blackmail.

I didn't want to see her upset and this conversation was clearly ruining her mood. I decided to change the subject. "I'm just thankful I found you to look after Ashley. I promise she's well-behaved."

Mary was quick to shake her head, obviously disagreeing with what I just said. "She's two. She shouldn't behave all the time. It's not a problem at all. I swear. I love kids, and I've already planned to take her to some parks and the science museum. I'm sure there's also more than enough time to take her to the zoo."

"Save the zoo for the weekend," I quickly piped up. "The three of us will go together."

I didn't miss the sneaky smirks that surfaced on

Jane's and Greg's faces. My friend looked at me and raised his eyebrow. Yeah, I was just as fucked as he was. No, I hoped to be getting fucked as much as he was. Soon. I just had to get Mary naked and beneath me, show her she was mine.

Jane started shaking her head as she looked from me to Mary. I knew what they were thinking. They put us together as employer and babysitter, but had they done a little matchmaking, too? I didn't care if they thought that. I just wanted Mary any way I could get her.

"We'll leave you two," said Greg, taking the dinner plates off the table and leaving the cheesecake. "I'm sure you want to come to an agreement before she starts sitting for Ashley. Jane and I will be in the kitchen."

Yeah, matchmaking. Worked for me. I had to remember to buy Greg a beer the next time we had a guy's night. I owed him one.

When the two of them left the room, I turned to face Mary, to give her my full attention. Our knees touched and she stared up at me with a mix of a smile and a smirk. With our closeness, I couldn't help but inhale her womanly scent, and I knew right then and there that I was a goner.

She might be my new babysitter, but there was no *fucking* way I'd be able to keep my hands off her.

2

Mary

I'D FINALLY FOUND *HIM* – THE GUY WHO WAS GOING TO take my virginity.

I'd begun to worry – that I'd go to college without ever going past second base. I didn't want to be the last of us among our friends to finally do it. To lose my V-card. Jane had succeeded with a home-run just a week after we graduated. She'd told me all about it. Well, *most* of it and I was so jealous. I'd lay in bed at night, touch myself and think of my own hot guy. A man who'd tell me what to do, to take me, fuck me, fill me. Night after night I dreamed of *the one* and now I'd found him.

It'd been a month since graduation. Aside from the

His Virgin Nanny

whole virgin thing, I just wanted to get away from my house because it felt like every time I was home, my stress levels were off the charts. My mom was to blame for everything. Going to the local college would've been much more affordable, but she was willing to pay thousands of dollars more per semester to have me across the country so she could have alone time with her new fiancé.

Yeah, the whole "that college has the best early education program" speech was bullshit. It wasn't as if I couldn't hear their mating calls from my bedroom. They didn't even care if I heard or saw everything they were doing. Dinner with those two was a nightmare. They were always feeling each other up, more than they would eat their food – and right in front of me.

I wanted out of the house as much as she wanted me gone, but I didn't need to go two time zones away to give them space. Going to dinner at Mr. Parker's house to meet a guy who needed a summer babysitter was great timing. I couldn't miss my mom leading Bob into her bedroom. Gag. But Jane had called and I'd accepted. I just had to remember that Mr. Parker wasn't my teacher anymore and I was supposed to call him Greg.

But I wasn't interested in Greg. I wanted Gabe. I wanted a man's touch. I wanted *his* touch. His kisses. His cock. I wanted him to claim me and fuck me. Gabe was practically God's gift to women with thick dark hair and soft, mesmerizing blue eyes. Not to mention his body...I'd thought Mr. Parker was one fit man and Jane always gushed about him, but the moment I saw Gabe, I tried my best not to let him see that my nipples were hard and I had to wonder if he knew that my panties were ruined after the first glance. I managed well, since I had the job.

After that, when Mr. Parker and Jane excused themselves to go to the kitchen, Gabe and I got down to business – but not *that* kind. He told me about my working hours – six hours a day – and how much he was paying – twenty dollars an hour. It was double what I would get working a retail job. I'd never worked before, and thankfully, I didn't have to, but having some experience, even babysitting, was always good for my resume. Not only that, but I really enjoyed kids. They were always so full of innocent energy, and a part of me missed that.

High school was all about pretending to know more than what we actually did. We couldn't let anyone know we were virgins. We pretended we were "too cool for school." We played games like Spin the Bottle and Truth or Dare as if we'd been playing it all our lives. Honestly, it was a breath of fresh air to be finally done with that. I just needed to lose my virginity before I went to college, or else I'd be back to square one and pretending I knew more than I did.

I took a left turn and drove further up the street until I saw his house number – sixty-nine. I couldn't help but smirk and start shaking my head when I saw it. I never even knew a house sign could make me feel so hot and horny. The idea of doing something like that with Gabe, well...I squirmed in my seat while pressing on the brakes and turning the engine off. I took my time getting out of my car and walking up to the front porch.

Gabe's house was easily a standout from all the others on the street, the subdivision even. Being an architect, there was no doubt that he put his time, effort, and imagination into creating the place of his dreams. From the floor-to-ceiling windows, to the wood and black iron detailing of the structure, the design was something I hadn't seen anywhere. Sure, it looked similar to those in high-end home magazines, but it wasn't anything like the carbon copy houses on the street.

He was so buff, probably because he was an architect – him being so fit, tanned, and muscular. I remembered Gabe mentioning during dinner how he had a few projects lined up and was constantly visiting sites to overlook the construction. My mind suddenly started to whip up thoughts of him carrying sacks of gravel or driving bulldozers and whatnot. I could picture him opting to go shirtless from the heat of the afternoon sun with beads of sweat trickling down his chiseled body. Lifting a sledgehammer, swinging it, muscles rippling.

Fuck. I was feeling hot and wet already. *Keep it together, woman*, I reminded myself. I was going to his place to babysit…not maul him. Well, at least not on the first day.

During the drive to Gabe's house, I felt both excited and nervous. I'd been trying to flirt with him that night we had dinner with Jane and Mr. Parker. I just hadn't been sure if he knew I was trying to get his attention. I'd catch him staring at me or glancing at my cleavage from time to time, but he never made any outright effort to take the sexual tension I was feeling a step further. Well, except that time he made me take a bite off his steak. He'd cut a piece for me and then fed me, and I remembered how close our faces were. I could see the brightness of his blue eyes and length of his eyelashes. They were unusually long for a guy, and it made him even more attractive.

"I heard your car pull up." The door opened before I even rang the doorbell. "Come in. Come in. You're right on time."

I nodded my head, smiled, and took a step inside his house. My shoulder slightly brushed against his chest, and I tried to keep my breathing even. My body was starting to feel warm, and the button down he donned wasn't helping. He looked like a *man*, so very different from the guys who went to the Catholic all-boys school we usually had dances and parties with. He wore a pair of dark washed jeans and a navy long-sleeved shirt. He paired the attire with leather brown loafers, and I swore I was going to come just looking at him. The shirt fit so well, being stretched across his toned chest.

His Virgin Nanny

It only accentuated and defined his strong arms and ripped abs.

"You're...come on, I'll introduce you to Ashley," he then said, turning around so that his back was facing me, as he started to walk down the hallway.

Automatically, I couldn't help but stick my bottom lip out into a pout and feel slightly disappointed. I felt a little bit rejected, or maybe he didn't know what I was trying to do? I was trying to get him to have sex with me, but he probably just saw me as an eighteen-year-old child. I cursed inwardly. *Fuck*, I needed to try harder.

I couldn't remain a virgin. I'd be a laughing stock in college.

The introduction with Ashley was...normal. At first, she was shy, hiding her face in her favorite blanket as she sat on the couch and watched Sesame Street. Only when I made some funny faces at her did she start to smile. When I asked Gabe the story of her parents, he said the father had left Gabe's sister while she was pregnant. Since Ashley was born, he'd been doing everything he could to help his sister with raising her child. I felt my heart tighten by the minute, seeing the way he loved his niece only made me see how he would be with other children. His own children, someday. That was another layer I hadn't known, and as we talked, I learned more about him. Finally, a few minutes passed and his phone began to ring. He ignored the call and then turned to me, although I could sense his mind beginning to be diverted toward work.

"I have to go to the office," he said, making a move to say goodbye to Ashley. After a hug and a kiss, he stood back up and came over to me. "You'll be alright?" he asked.

I nodded and crossed my arms again. I couldn't miss the way he glanced at my breasts, but he did nothing about it. Said nothing. I only saw the heat in his eyes. Not that he would do more in front of his niece. "My number's on the fridge if you need to call me. Emergency info, too."

Oh. "Got it. We're good here, right Ash?" I asked, grinning at the little girl. She didn't know what we were talking about, but she seemed fine with me.

With another nod, he finally left the room. Not long after, I heard the sound of a car engine turning on, and then, he was off. I went to sit beside Ashley on the couch and we watched a few minutes of Sesame Street in silence. Only when the credits rolled did she mutter something incoherent as she pointed to the colorful building blocks stacked on the top shelf of the family room built-ins. I reached for them and set the pieces on the floor. She came over and began to build what looked like a rectangular, three-floored tower.

The day went fine after that. After several hours of playing, she became fussy and went down for a long nap. As she slept, I thought about what was going to

His Virgin Nanny

happen when Gabe came home. The hours passed in what felt like forever.

The days with Ashley after that fell into a routine, the hours alternating between playing and learning. I felt she knew more than I did when I was her age. She could match shapes, colors, and numbers, and she was quick to label certain body parts from a children's book. When it came to fun, there were building blocks, jumbo-sized legos, and the backyard inflatable pool to choose from.

I hadn't seen much of Gabe other than a quick hello at the door before he left for work or a "Thanks" at the door before I went home. Three days of simple pleasantries. Three days with nothing but heated stares from Gabe. Nothing more. If he didn't make a move soon, I was going to combust.

I knew he wanted me, knew there was chemistry between us. If he wasn't going to move things along, then I was. Was I being bold? Yes. Desperate times called for desperate measures. I was *not* going to college a virgin. So when I got dressed this morning, I decided on a plaid skirt – not my old school uniform – and a tank top. I debated whether to leave the house with my bra on or off and went for the latter.

Gabe always eyed my breasts. He wasn't sleazy about it, but I couldn't miss it. And he wouldn't miss the way my hardened nipples tried to poke out of the thin material of my top. For a second, I thought it'd be too much. I was going over to babysit...but I also wanted to seduce him. I wasn't going to spend the summer waiting for him to make a move. No, if I wanted his cock buried deep inside my needy pussy, I needed to make it clear.

"Fake it 'til you make it," I whispered to myself. I had zero experience when it came to sex. My only sexual adventure was kissing other girls during parties. It was fun, safe, and a little hot even, and the guys – well, boys who watched – always loved it. I'd had a few of them come on to me, but I'd never gotten wet for any of them. Never wanted them to touch me and never considered one of them to be the one to take my virginity. No, I wanted that for someone special.

For Gabe.

But those had all been boys. They all acted immaturely and just talked a big game. I had a feeling they held off doing anything because they didn't actually know what to do. With Gabe, I figured he was holding off because I was too young. I wasn't too young. Well, I didn't think he was too old.

I bit my bottom lip. I knew my reputation at the private school. Everyone had thought I was *so* experienced because I'd always gave tips and advice I'd read off the internet. I knew what to do when it came to sex, be it oral, vaginal, or anal. I'd watched enough porn, but I was just hoping expectation was close to reality.

Fake it 'til you make it, my inner voice repeated in my head, and I gave myself a nod of confidence. I needed that especially later if I was going to get Gabe to see me as more than just the summer babysitter and finally take my virginity.

No bra then.

I boldly tossed the lace back onto my bed. I gave myself one last look in the mirror, more than satisfied with how I looked. My skirt was short and flirty. The nude, lace thong beneath made it look like I wasn't wearing any underwear, if he ever flipped up skirt. My nipples were hard and perky, and my breasts were large and full enough to be flush against my tank top.

Perfect.

I was dressed to kill, or rather, I was dressed to have sex.

When Gabe opened the door for me this morning, I couldn't miss how his eyes immediately went to my breasts and he inhaled ever so slightly. I couldn't miss it. He looked curiously at me, questioning, probably wanting to know why I wasn't wearing a bra. I hadn't been bold, until now. I crossed my arms and rested them below my breasts to deepen my cleavage. Yeah, that was bold.

He coughed loudly, clearing his throat. "I'm late," he murmured, grabbing his briefcase. "Ashley's in the book corner." He dashed out then, one last glance at me, then raking down my body before he shut the door behind him.

When I heard the door open that night, it was a few minutes after seven and Ashley was fast asleep in her toddler bed. I was in the kitchen washing the dinner dishes.

"Oh," Gabe said, stepping inside from the garage. Obviously, he was at a loss for words.

It wasn't my fault. He'd caught me by surprise. I was bent over, loading the bottom rack of the dishwasher. I instantly stood up, realizing my skirt had ridden up and he could see my bare bottom and the little line of my thong. I almost dropped a plate on the floor, and apologized to him. So much for seducing him. What man gets turned on by a woman filling a dishwasher?

The next words out of his mouth shocked me…but in a good way. "There's nothing to apologize for."

3

abe

She was doing it on purpose. I *fucking* knew it. It was the first time she wasn't wearing a fucking bra, but she'd been taunting me with her perky tits and smooth thighs ever since the night we met.

I wasn't going to pretend I was a saint. I *fucking* loved it every time Mary displayed that full ass of hers and slender legs. And the way her nipples poked against her thin tank top? Yeah, I was an asshole for staring, but I was only a man. A horny man with fucking blue balls.

School was already over, high school a thing of the

past for her, but she'd still come to babysit Ashley wearing a short skirt that reminded me of her old uniform. My mind was telling me to stay away, and I'd been able to do it up until now, but my dick was hard every time I saw her. Hard? No, it was a steel beam in my pants.

It was the third time this week I came home to her sashaying her hips. The first night, she'd been in the living room with the vacuum turned on, rocking those lush hips to the music she had coming through her ear buds. I thought I'd blow my load then and there.

Tonight? She'd added the flirty fucking skirt to her teasing. And she'd worn a damn white tank top and I could see her hard nipples peeking through. I could even see they were dark pink. *Fuck.*

I tried and succeeded in not groaning out loud. I would've ravaged her right then and there, but I didn't think she'd like that. Hell, I'd had to storm out of the house this morning or I would have taken her. She wouldn't want an older man like me. I'd questioned it for days. But now? Now maybe she would…

She *would*…if the way she stared at my erection and licked her bottom lip was any indication. If her nipples were like pencil erasers. If her skirt wasn't practically showing off her pert ass.

"Ashley's asleep?" I confirmed. If I was going to make Mary mine, I wanted Ashley sound asleep. No interruptions for what I wanted to do to Mary.

"You know it," she said. "I took her to the country

club today and she played for hours in the wading pool. I can see her becoming an Olympic swimmer. She's a natural."

At the exact same time, we stared at each other and burst out laughing. Looking at her, I couldn't help but shake my head. From the way she spoke and moved, she was the perfect combination of youthful and sexy. She wasn't just a pretty face with a body I'd like to fuck. She had a personality that could light up any room, and it was such a turn-on that the thought of her voice made my erection harder, if that was even still possible.

"Enough about Ashley," I said, moving closer to her.

I raised my hand up to tuck a strand of her hair behind her ear before grazing my fingers over her cheek. Her flesh was soft and so smooth against my own, like a woman's, and I *loved* women. I loved how they felt so small and little beside me. But none of them had been Mary. The past women I'd dated never failed to mention how they always felt so safe and secure with me, like I would protect them from any harm. It was true. I would never hurt a woman, never see one hurt by someone else. I was a gentleman.

With the way she stared up at me, I could tell Mary felt the same. She liked the feeling of standing beside me and feeling small. She wanted that feeling. She wanted me to protect her. I'd never thought about it before, but thinking now, I realized I didn't mind. There was just something about her that wanted me to get to know her better, to know her likes and dislikes, what turned her on and what turned her off. I wanted to know how she would be in bed, and when I thought like that, I wasn't a gentleman at all. I wanted to know everything.

I wanted to know if she blushed everywhere. I wanted to know if she was as wet as I suspected. I wanted to know the sounds she made when I slipped my fingers into her for the first time, put my mouth on her pussy, filled her with my huge dick. I wanted to know what she looked like when she came.

Yeah, that was my dick talking. It could make all my life's decisions for me; it'd never failed me before. I wouldn't think it'd fail me now with Mary. Looking at her with her breasts flushed against my chest, her nipples poking me, I could never fathom how she would ever be a wrong decision. She was the whole package – face, body, and brains. That already made her rare amongst the female population, and I knew that population quite well.

She bit her lip, looked up at me through her fringed lashes.

I was the one who took a step back, but my eyes remained on hers. Pinned her in place.

"Come," I then said, leading her out of the kitchen and to the couch in the great room, and she followed suit. "You've been a bad girl, haven't you, Mary?"

I saw the way her eyes widened instantly and she froze. I hurriedly opened my mouth and explained, making sure she didn't get the wrong expression. "The

His Virgin Nanny

way you're seducing me, aren't you?" were the first words that left my mouth. "Being a naughty girl by showing me your ass and thong. Those hard nipples. A bad girl, aren't you?"

I was shocked when she curved her lips upwards into a knowing smile, then nodded her head.

"Why?"

She was young and gorgeous and could have any guy she wanted. Why was she seducing a thirty-year-old man?

Her pink tongue flicked out and licked her lower lip. "Because I want you to take my virginity."

Take her virginity? Fuck. My dick went rock hard, as if it wasn't already.

"I would've never guessed..." It was my turn to smirk. "Although Greg did mention a bunch of his students making a pact to lose their virginity before college, like his Jane. You're one of them, huh?"

"Are we just going to keep talking?" she asked, putting her finger to her lip.

Damn. She never failed to surprise me. Up until she arrived this morning, I could have imagined her a virgin. But today? Her outfit, her hard nipples, her heated gazes said experience. I would never have expected that kind of confidence in an eighteen-year-old, much less one who was a virgin. But I liked this dichotomy. Vixen and virgin in one. Somehow, she was pushing all of the right buttons. I wouldn't even be surprised if I came in my pants just from her talking. I was so wound up thinking about her pert tits all day.

"You're an impatient girl, aren't you?" I said with a teasing grin. "Naughty and impatient…" I said that more to myself than to her. She'd just taken me by surprise with her confidence and boldness. I fucking *loved* it. And I was going to love fucking her.

"Well, I've been waiting for eighteen years. I think I've waited long enough."

"You think you can handle my cock taking that virgin pussy?" Yes, she'd be able to handle it. The fit would be tight. Her pussy would be so fucking tight, but I'd fit. She was made to take me.

The rules had changed. Right now, I was no longer her boss and she was no longer my babysitter. No, she was the woman I was going to fuck. She wanted it and wasn't hiding that in the least, especially with her nipples pointing straight at me. I wasn't hiding anything either, as I slid my hand underneath my jeans and rubbed my dick right in front of her. My cock was happy to be stroked, but would only be satisfied buried deep in that hot, wet channel.

Her eyes widened with what I was doing, and I noticed how she'd started squirming where she stood and how her breathing turned ragged. It was good to know I wasn't the only one feeling horny. I knew where this would lead. She was the virgin. She might have started this, but there was no doubt she wanted me to finish it.

Pulling my hand out of my jeans, I stepped up to her and slid it underneath her skirt to rub her bare ass. She lifted her bum a bit, and I continued to move my hand up and down her smooth flesh. It was hot and smooth, tight and pert. Perfect.

"So you want me to fuck you?" I asked her, throwing away all pretenses. She'd been seducing me all along. I was no martyr. It was only a matter of time until I broke down and succumbed to her, and that moment was right now. She nodded her head and maintained eye contact. *Yes, fuck me.* She basically told me with the intensity in her emerald eyes. "How come no one has ever fucked your virgin pussy before?"

With her eyes on mine, she shrugged.

"Has anyone touched you?" I asked curiously, and when she moved her head to say *no*, I wrapped a strong arm around her waist, tugged her to sit on my lap on the couch. I didn't settle her toward me, but so she looked out at the room. She glanced once at me over her shoulder, then looked away.

I couldn't help it, my hands explored the expanse of her flesh, as they slid down past her perky nipples to rest on her inner thighs. Just the smallest of movements and I'd be right at her entrance, my hands ready to take her. I suddenly had the brilliant idea to test myself – how long it would take before I lost all control. My dick didn't like the idea, but he wasn't in charge. This was her first time and I wanted her so revved up she'd come before I even got inside her.

Leaning her back so she rested against my chest to practically lay on top of me, I flipped her skirt up, exposing her pathetic excuse of a flimsy thong to reveal a thin strip of trimmed hair covering a thin line above her pussy. "Fuck, baby. You're dripping."

The string of her thong was marred with her own juices and I felt my dick jerk against my pants. Against her ass. So much for testing myself. With her on my lap, she spread her legs wide open and rested the soles of her feet on the edge of the couch. Oh yeah, my girl was eager.

"You like that, huh?" I asked when Mary started moaning as my fingers slid up and down the plump lips of her pussy. They were getting soaked, and I was ecstatic. She was just as eager as me. Just as needy and not even a single part of me was inside her…yet. "Oh, fucking hell…moan any louder, and you're gonna make me cum in my pants."

"Gabe," she breathed, voice becoming hoarse. "Hmmm…"

She let her head fall backward over my left shoulder as she arched her back, her perky breasts pointing towards the ceiling. Her eyes slipped closed as her hips moved. Her straight white teeth bit into her lower lip. She was gorgeous with her desire. Passionate. Easily aroused. Perfect.

Her plaid skirt pooled around her waist, and I impatiently tugged at the thin string of her lace panties and ripped them off. The small scrap of fabric was redolent with her scent and ruined with her arousal. I tossed it onto the floor. She started to thrust her hips toward the ceiling as two of my fingers began to draw invisible circles on her clit. It poked out, swollen and eager, just for me.

"Finger me, *please*," she begged, and I felt a surge of pride run through my veins. She was so naughty, so bold.

I'd give her what she wanted, this time, but she'd soon learn who was in charge. I slipped two fingers inside her and began to carefully work them in and out, avoiding that thin membrane that proved her virginity. I was going to tear through that, but with my cock. Her breathing became ragged as I took my sweet time exploring her internal walls. This was her first time. She needed to experience the best and I was going to give it to her.

Careful not to finger fuck her too deep, I folded my fingers into the shape of a hook to reach a different part of her, that swollen ridge of flesh that made her purr. Her eyes flew open and when I started to move them in and out again, keeping the curled position, her moans turned into screams, and she started to shiver against me. Holy hell, she was so responsive. With her thrusting her hips, she was unknowingly rubbing my dick. I wouldn't be surprised if we finished together, and that was with my pants *on*. I knew pre-cum stained the front of them. I was too eager for her.

"I'm gonna come, Gabe...I'm gonna come," she

moaned, and right then and there, I pulled my fingers out of her.

She whimpered, then arched her back. Unfulfilled. That's right. I'd make her come, but I wanted her to know it would be with my dick deep inside her.

Yeah, I wasn't done with her yet. I'd only just begun.

4

"Not yet, little girl. You don't get to come yet. You've been taunting me these past few days..." Gabe began, as he lifted me off his lap to stand, then turned me so our eyes met. "Such a bad girl."

I towered over him, yet I kept my gaze turned down and I felt so small before him. His knees were spread, and I could see his erection trying to burst out of his pants. He rubbed his hand up and down his groin, stroking his manhood, but his azure eyes never left mine.

With every passing second, I could feel the aching need in my pussy. After he'd been rubbing my clit and fingering me impatiently, all I wanted was his full dick inside me, thrusting in and out until I screamed his name. I'd almost come and that had just been from his fingers. I touched myself to get off, but it had never been like this. I shouldn't have told him I was on the verge of finishing. *Damn it.* Because then he wouldn't have pulled his fingers out and stopped assaulting my clit, and now, I'd have to wait, and I was an impatient girl.

"Stand in the corner and show me that ass of yours," he said, reaching around to rub the cheeks of my bum. My skirt had fallen back over it, but it seemed almost illicit to have him cup me from beneath.

"B-But…" I began, confusion and disappointment tingeing my voice. "I-I t-thought…" *I thought we were going to have sex! Wasn't that the obvious next step after fingering?*

He slapped me on the ass with his big palm. He *fucking* spanked it. And it felt so goddamn good. The sharp sting, the way it morphed into heat.

"I'm going to teach you the value of patience, my little tease," he said, his hand still stroking my behind. I was hotter and wetter with every stroke and touch. That feeling in my pussy was building up again, and it was just getting to be too much to handle…but in a *very* good way. I squirmed before him. I liked–*loved*–what was happening. It was so much different from masturbating and pleasuring myself. Yes, I got wet and hot each time, but the excitement and thrill of being controlled weren't there. And Gabe was really controlling me. The corner?

I wanted him to fuck me already, but he wouldn't. I wanted him to eat me out, he'd be really good at it, his tongue and mouth on my pussy. I wanted to strip him of his clothes and see his naked body, to see what his dick looked like, to see how big it was. Judging from the strain in his pants, it was huge and it was going to rip me in two. I wanted sex. I didn't want to be a virgin anymore. I wanted to finish and come. I wanted all of that but I fucking had to wait. He didn't want this to be about taking my V-card. No, he was making this about so much more or we would have been done by now.

And for some weird reason, I liked the feeling of not getting what I wanted. I liked the feeling of doing what Gabe said. Of listening to his authority.

It wasn't like my mother paid me any mind. And my father? He'd been gone since I was two. Aside from wanting to go to the local college instead of the one across the country my mother picked, I'd always gotten what I wanted. So had my mother.

I wasn't going to embellish things. My mother was a whore. She was gorgeous, even for her age, and used it to her advantage. She had men – rich men – following her like a lost puppy. They always knew she was after their money, and yet, they'd commit to her. She must have been really good in bed in trade. Something. She milked them for all they had, and every time I benefited from my mother's hard work. I was sent to the best schools and had everything I needed and wanted. Overseas vacations were the norm, and having the latest product and trendiest wardrobe were a must. For once, right now, I wasn't getting what I wanted – to be fucked – and I felt thrilled hearing a "no" for the first time. And from a guy like Gabe? It made it hot.

After a long stretch of silence, Gabe squeezed my ass and just arched a brow. I stepped back, did what I was told. I walked over to one end of the living room and stood in the corner.

"Lift the skirt. Higher, higher and show me that ass. Good girl. Hold it up high and don't let that skirt drop." I sucked in a breath at his direction. I felt my cheeks heat and my juices slide down my thighs. I wanted to wipe it away since I knew he could see it, but I didn't dare lower my arms.

I'd teased him and gotten myself into this position, but I was a virgin. I'd never done anything like this before. I might've talked a big game, but the truth was, I didn't know what to do.

Should I start stripping or giving him a lap dance?

Does he want me to show more than just my ass?

Do I crawl closer to him again after he'd just told me to stand in the corner?

I was getting more nervous by the second. He probably sensed what I was feeling because he said, "I like seeing your ass, baby girl…that big round ass of yours…"

I couldn't see his face, only the smooth white wall. My back was to him, but I noticed the tone of mischief in his voice. His voice was cool and collected, and yet, I could hear just a tinge of excitement in it. He knew what was going to happen later on, but somehow he could wait for it, could punish me instead of pleasuring us both.

"Put your hands on the wall and bend at the waist. Stick that ass out so I can see all of it. All of you."

I did what I was told. I put my palms on the cool wall and bent forward. With one hand, I flipped up my skirt that had slid back down with my movements and gave him a view of my naked ass. Not just my ass, but I knew my pussy was on complete display. If he had any doubts about my eagerness for him, he would know now. With my head low, I could see him between my two legs, sitting on the couch, eyes on me as he stroked his dick. He'd taken it out of his pants while my back had been turned, and I couldn't miss how well-endowed he was. It was a dark plum color, a pulsing vein along the length of the shaft. His fist gripped it tightly and slid up and down. The flared head was bulbous and I watched as clear fluid seeped from the little slit at the tip. He used his thumb to slide over that pre-cum and coat himself with it. It was the first time I'd seen a dick in real life, and my pussy muscles automatically clenched. I felt so much hotter and wetter, if those were still possible even, and I almost lost my balance with the pool of heat building up inside me. I wanted that monster in me. Stretching me. Filling me deep.

"Show me how you touch yourself, Mary…" he said to me, his hand still moving up and down his length. "What do you do when you're all alone?"

I sucked in a long, heavy breath and placed two fingers over my clit. Still bent forward, I began to rub them in small circles as my free hand was against the wall to support myself.

"Ah, ah," he chided. "Don't put your fingers in your pussy. That's just for me now. My fingers go there. My fingers give you that pleasure. Or my cock. Nothing else. Say it."

"Your fingers. Your cock," I breathed, getting closer to coming.

"That's right. That's my pussy now, isn't it?"

"Your pussy," I repeated. My hand needed to stay propped against the wall or else I wouldn't be standing upright any longer.

"Hmmm…so you like to play with yourself, huh?" he said in a teasing tone. "Is that what they taught you in your Catholic school?" When I shook my head, Gabe continued with, "I think I need to punish you…I'll make a good girl out of you yet."

With my fingers still rubbing my clit, I breathed, "I thought guys liked bad girls? Aren't good girls boring?"

From where I stood, I could see the immediate grin on his face. He started shaking his head from side to side. It took him a while to respond. "But good girls get what they want…and didn't you want to lose your virginity?"

"Yes," I said quickly, almost too eagerly.

"Are you going to be a good girl tonight? Are you going to stop teasing me and behave?"

I nodded my head, but not before I said, "I don't know. Do good girls get to sit on Daddy's lap?"

Still bent over, I saw the way his eyes widened. I stopped fingering myself, wanting him to make me come, and watched him keenly. He was probably shocked at my question, and how I had zero hesitation in asking it and calling him "Daddy." Sometimes, I just really surprised myself.

I wanted him to take care of me, to discipline me, to put me in the corner when I needed it. I wanted his guidance, especially when it came to fucking.

"Come here, little girl," he finally told me. He'd stop stroking himself, but his legs were still spread and his dick stood hard and tall unashamedly. I couldn't wait to get a taste of that, to feel it inside me. Jane told me how her first time had hurt and that she bled a little, but Greg had taken good care of her. Would the same thing happen to me? I couldn't think about that, not now. I'd been playing the seductive card so well despite my nerves all on overdrive.

Finally, I stood and took a moment – I'd been bent forward for far too long – before I walked over to Gabe. I took my sweet time, a little nervous about what would come next. He was right. I'd been taunting him the past couple of days. It was the only way I was going to get what I wanted. He was just too *good*. I'd needed to seduce him if I wanted him to take my virginity. I couldn't pretend to be all innocent and angelic and wait for sex to come to me. I believed opportunities didn't fall on people's laps. Opportunities were made – just as what mother did. She wanted a rich man to give her the high-flying life? She made the opportunity by always staying gorgeous no matter her age.

I wanted to lose my virginity with Gabe? I made the opportunity and seduced him so he'd see me as a woman and not a girl. Even though he called me *little girl*, he didn't make me feel like one.

"Are you comfortable?" he asked when I sat on his lap. Well, it was more like I was straddling him with my knees splayed on either side of his hips. I frowned a bit when I realized he'd zipped his pants back up, and his dick was nowhere in sight anymore. The only sign was the hard bump underneath the denim. Why had he put it away?

"I am..." I responded with a nod, bit my lip. "You hid your dick again..."

"I did." There was no missing the mischief lacing his voice, the way his dark eyes held mine. "Didn't I tell you good girls needed to be patient?" I nodded my head for the second time. "It'll be inside you in no time, little girl. Splitting open that virgin pussy, filling you so deep you'll have to wiggle your pert little ass to get me to fit."

At that, I couldn't help but inhale sharply and crash my lips against his. I couldn't wait any longer. With every minute passing, I was growing wetter and wetter to the point that I was scared I wouldn't be able to handle what I was feeling inside, and I'd be a writhing mess in front of him. He knew how to turn me on. God, did he. I'd been wet ever since the first time I met him at Greg's house for dinner.

Even better, he knew how to work the foreplay. He'd tease me repeatedly and get me on the verge of finishing, just to do a one-eighty and pull back. A few minutes ago, he was fingering me and about to make me come, then he put me in the corner only to have me play with myself. And now, we were back to the beginning with us making out. No cock in sight.

I wasn't going to hide the truth. I never did. I was an impatient girl, and he must've realized that when I started thrusting and grinding as I straddled him, my slender legs caging his thick, muscular ones. All throughout, he was responsive. Even better, he did so eagerly and with the same amount of impatience I had. His hands roamed to explore every inch of my flesh and he'd tugged my tank top out of my skirt so that his hands could snake underneath to touch my breasts. To cup them, let them fill his palms

"That feels so good…" I said with closed eyes, as I moved my lips from his mouth to his neck. When I bit into his skin, he pulled away slightly and started shaking his head. "Not tonight, Mary." Despite the rejection, his lips were curved up into a boyish smile. It was adorable, seeing such a sheepish grin on a man like him.

"I have work tomorrow…I can't have any hickeys. What will my clients think? I can't tell them you were a bad girl and made marks on me."

I thought of saying something naughty, something along the lines of he didn't need to care about what they thought and that they'd probably be even jealous that he was getting some action. Instead, I reminded myself that I was a good girl, or at least playing the part. I wanted to be just what he wanted.

"Okay, I'll be a good girl," I said with the most angelic smirk…if smirks could even be angelic ever.

"Perfect," came his smiling response. "And you know daddies give good girls prizes, don't you?"

"Really?" I was still straddling him and he was still cupping my breasts, his fingers playing and tugging on my nipples, but we'd finally stopped kissing. "What do good girls get?"

The next few seconds were the most intense I'd ever felt. I could see him staring at me, trying to read me, and I was doing the same thing to him. I didn't know what he felt, but I went into this wanting an attractive man to de-virginize me. No, not just an attractive man. Him. I wanted Gabe.

He wasn't just a stranger who was going to fuck me. The more I got to know him and spend time with him and his niece, the more I wanted to be in his life, even after we'd have sex. One time wasn't going to be enough.

"They get a big, hard cock, nice and deep in that perfect, untried pussy. They get a load of hot cum filling them up. And they get to scream with pleasure as they get it. Is that something you want or do you want to stand in the corner again?"

I licked my lips with anticipation. "I want you to take my virginity, to fill me up, nice and deep."

His eyes never left mine, but I heard a growl rumble deep in his chest. After what felt like an eternity, he finally nodded his head. "Are you on birth control?" he asked. "I want nothing between us. When I fuck you, I'll take you raw, deep and bare."

I almost breathed out a sigh of relief for having the right answer because I wanted that, too. I nodded my head. "I've had the shot."

It was Gabe's turn to suck in a long, heavy breath as his hand cupped my left breast. Pinched the nipple and making me gasp. "Perfect. I'll meet you in my bedroom. I'll go check on Ashley first and make sure she's fast asleep. Know this, little girl, I won't be fucking you right away. I have some other things to show you first."

I did as I was told, just as I'd been doing the past days in Gabe's house. Whatever he asked, whether it was taking Ashley somewhere or running a quick household errand for him, I did it eagerly and with zero hesitation. None of it felt forced. I wanted to please him and I was especially going to do so tonight.

As I walked away from him and toward the staircase, I could feel his eyes burning into the back of me. *This* was finally happening. I was going to have sex for the first time. I was going to take his big cock inside me. I was going to be a good girl and feel every inch of his cock, latex-free as it filled my pussy with all his cum. He was so virile I knew it was going to be a lot. So much that it would slide down my thighs, coat me inside and out.

I was both nervous and scared. But I couldn't wait any longer. *Finally*. There was no turning back, and as I walked to the master bedroom, I couldn't help the smile that spread across on my face.

5

ary

HE WAS INSIDE ME, INSIDE MY MOUTH. SO THIS WAS what it felt like…sucking dick…and I *loved* it.

Seriously, I could stare at it – him – all day. Look up at the tense lines of his face from my position on my knees before him. It wasn't just because of his size though, both length or girth…that would take a whole day to rave about. Every part of his penis was perfectly shaped, even its texture inside my mouth was a feeling I couldn't get over. The tip was just so soft. It felt so delicate, but all the rest of him was the complete opposite, rock hard. His erection felt like steel against my hand and it dug in and out of my mouth like a drill.

I couldn't help the gagging noises as the tip darted again inside me, poking my throat. He probably must have been all the more turned on with the sounds if the way he grabbed fistfuls of my hair was any indication.

He was careful, yet pushed me. At first, I'd thought there was no way I could swallow all of him, but little by little, he'd gone deeper. Saliva dripped down my chin and I breathed his muskiness through my nose.

"Such a good cock sucker for Daddy."

Him fingering me, me pleasuring myself for his private viewing, and him planting a trail of warm kisses all over my skin, it all felt so great, but me sucking him was a whole other level. It piqued my interest when it came to sex. To the intimacy of it. The power behind the actions. While I was on my knees, I definitely took some of his control as soon as I took his cock into the back of my throat. And his arousal only fueled mine.

Patience, I reminded myself. *Good girls get rewarded.*

His hands rested against each side of my face, a firm cup against my cheeks, as he continued to thrust his dick in and out my mouth. His head fell backwards as he let out a series of roaring groans. He sounded primal and hungry, like the true Alpha that he was, the more I felt my pussy turn wet. I was ready for him, more than ready, and I could tell he was as well.

Slowly, he pulled himself out of my mouth and stared at me from head to toe.

"I'm not coming in that mouth, you tease. You

His Virgin Nanny

might be able to suck the cum from my balls, but I want it deep in that pussy of yours, not your belly. Lose the top, little girl."

I still had my tank top on but he'd tugged it up above my breasts so he could watch them as I sucked him off. Now, it must have been distracting for him, so I pulled it over my head, dropped it to the floor. My skirt had been discarded a long time ago, and now I was fully naked in front of him, kneeling at his feet. Before his cock. Waiting for my next instructions.

"You want to please Daddy, don't you?"

I nodded.

"Up on the bed then. Crawl, little girl."

I shuddered with desire at his deep voice, his commands. I felt a little like a slut. His slut. While he wanted me to be a good girl, I felt very, very bad. But what Daddy wanted, Daddy got so I crawled toward the bed, then on it, ass in full view, breasts swinging as I moved, all the while he watched, dick out, but otherwise fully clothed.

I turned around and rested my back against headboard and waited for him. With a simple arch of a brow, he told me what he wanted, that he was waiting for me. I spread my legs widely, my pussy open and ready for him, weeping and begging desperately to be taken.

Gabe's fingers grabbed the hem of his shirt and he pulled the material over his head. His jeans pooled around his ankles and he kicked them away until all I could see was bare flesh. I sucked in a breath. This was the first time I'd seen him completely naked – all of him. Any man. He was my first in so many ways. The suits and long sleeves he wore did such a great job at hiding his physique. He was leanly muscled, like a swimmer or a runner, but he was in no way scrawny or lanky either. His skin was defined by hard, sinewy lines beneath.

It sounded stupid, but the only adjective I could think of was that he was hard, not only down *there*, but everywhere. From his arms to his legs and even his chest and abs, he was strength personified. Maybe it was an architect thing. He was always talking about how he would visit construction sites and get to work. Being under the hot sun with a sledgehammer hardened him, and I wasn't complaining.

My mind was brought back to reality when he crawled up onto the bed and his hands started to roam my flesh. I shivered slightly at his touch. No man had ever touched me the way he was doing at the moment. I loved the feel of large, warm hands against my soft skin. It was a new feeling, definitely, one I would need to get used to still.

"Are you sure you want to do this?" he asked, searching my eyes.

He'd been in control the whole time, telling me what to do, instructing me how I was going to pleasure myself and him. Even guiding me on how to suck his cock. But fucking my virgin pussy was something else entirely.

It was different to hear him ask me for consent, and I wasn't going to deny that him asking me thawed my heart. It endeared him more to me. He dominated and controlled, but I knew the whole time he was still looking out for me, making sure I agreed and wanted all that we'd done and were about to do. That's why I called him Daddy. He was everything I was looking for in a man, everything who understood me and my needs, both physically and emotionally.

A second or two passed before I finally gathered the courage to say what was on my mind. I could've easily given him some quick, unthought-of reply, but there was just something about the moment that pressed me to lay my feelings on the line. "I couldn't think of anyone else I'd rather do it with. Fuck me, Daddy."

I saw the grin that surfaced on his face when I said those words, and I couldn't help but return it with a smile of my own. He settled himself between my thighs, gripped a hip to hold me open.

Right then and there, I felt his tip brushing against my entrance. His eyes held mine as I felt him enter me, one slow inch at a time. He was big. He did stretch me wide. Filled me like I never could have imagined.

"Daddy," I breathed, then began to pant as he went even deeper.

"Such a good girl. That's it. I'm filling you up."

Jane was right, it hurt at first. I couldn't open my

eyes as I tried to get used to the feeling. Gabe handled it so much better than I ever expected, that he was fucking someone who had no idea what she was doing. I expected him to have given up, to tell me that maybe tonight wasn't going to work out, that he didn't want to waste his time with a virgin when he could get with more experienced women who didn't bleed or were in pain during sex. He did none of that.

What he did was made sure with every inch of him I took that I was adjusting, that I was taking him easily enough. I was wet, that wasn't a concern. But I was tight. Really tight.

"You're so big."

"Too big?" he asked, his voice rough.

I shook my head, pressed down on him a little bit more. Then more still and I could feel myself getting wetter and wetter with his dick bottoming out inside me.

With one surprise move, he flipped me over so I was astride him. The soft hair on my legs tickling me, I met his gaze.

"I took all of you," I said, surprised and pleased, wiggling my hips a bit to adjust to this new position.

He grinned. "You did. You took all of your Daddy's dick. Now take it for a ride. Up and down. That's it. I want to watch you."

Putting my hands on his shoulders, I lifted and lowered myself, impaling my pussy on him again and again. I watched Gabe, his eyes transfixed on my

His Virgin Nanny

breasts. They were bouncing and swaying with my motions and when I ground down on him so my clit got rubbed, he leaned forward and took a nipple into his mouth.

When he bit it gently, I came, milking him.

"Fuck, little girl, I'm going to come." He hardened within me, then spurt hotly. I could feel each burst of his cum filling me right up.

I was sweaty and messy as I tried to pull off him. Just as I imagined, his cum seeped out and covered both our thighs. Tinged with red, it showed what he'd done. Fucked me for the first time. Made me his. Placing his hands on my hips, he held me in place.

"Let Daddy stay inside you for another minute. It's not every day I take my little girl's cherry."

Leaning in, I kissed him, pleased he'd been my first. I went home that night with Gabe's cum still dripping from my bare pussy and down my thighs. I refused to take a shower, reveling in his possession marking me all hot and sticky.

―――

THE NEXT MORNING, I DIDN'T WANT TO WAKE UP. I dreamed about Gabe, his hands, his mouth, the feeling of him inside me – my first sex. It was all I wanted to think about, but I was woken up by my mother yelling at me with a bunch of flyers in her hand.

"Why are we getting mail from the local college?"

she asked, tugging open my blinds and sitting on the side of my bed.

I let out a groan and tried to cover my eyes from the bright light. I'd gotten home late, and I hadn't fallen asleep right away. I probably only had five hours of sleep and I didn't need my mother yelling in my ear. She didn't care that I was late last night, that I'd fucked my boss or that I'd even lost my virginity. She cared about local college flyers because it might mess with her.

"I signed up for the newsletter…" I didn't want to sit up and engage. I didn't want to talk and fight with her. I just wanted to dream and think of Gabe. I could feel the soreness between my legs. His cock had been huge inside me and I wasn't used to it. I was achy where he'd torn through my hymen and I felt dried cum on my thighs. For a moment, I forgot what we were talking about, but when I saw her irate expression, I focused on her, not my fabulously used pussy. "I didn't know they were going to mail me."

"Didn't we already talk about this? The best program for you is at the school across the country. Why are you giving up your future and staying here? Do you want me to fend for you until you're old? Is that it?" She threw the flyers on my bed and glared at me. "I've provided you a great life and gave you everything you needed and wanted. Mary, I can't do that forever. You're going to have to be independent one day, and that will start at the end of the summer when you get to college."

I didn't realize how quickly my mood could turn sour until this moment.

"I know, Mom." I tried my best not to roll my eyes in front of her. "I'm not saying I'm not going to go to college. I want to stay here because it's more affordable for me. That's what you want, right? For me to be smart? To live on my own? I know you'll be paying for my tuition if I go to that other school, but what about my living expenses? I'd have to find a job, and that's not even sure. Here, I can continue to work for Gabe and babysit Ashley. It would be flexible and it would pay my expenses. I wouldn't have to worry about applying to jobs here since I already have one. I won't have to depend on you."

That got her to shut up. She wasn't expecting that. My mother thought I was an idiot, who only depended on my looks to get by. Thought a job as a pre-school teacher was stupid. I wasn't like her. With my response, she couldn't help but zip her mouth shut. She didn't know what to say because I was right. I had a job with Gabe. At least until Ashley's mom returned, but then maybe I could work for her.

Soon after, she turned and walked out of the room. That was the end of it, at least for the moment, but I just couldn't stop thinking about what just happened. My mother and I were…civil. That was the best way to put it. She had been so busy with her new fiancé that we barely spoke and hung out. She didn't want me around, that was obvious. I had to wonder if she even loved me. I was more like a boarder in the house than a daughter. Maybe it was time to leave. It was getting toxic. She was toxic. I needed fresh air. I needed space. I needed Gabe.

6

*abe*

I COULDN'T WAIT TO SEE HER – MARY. AFTER LAST night, I couldn't get her out of my head.

Jesus. Her pussy, her nipples, her little moans. The way she came and clenched my dick like a vise. The way she called me Daddy.

I'd never been into that kind of shit before, but with her, it just seemed right. She needed some authority, some dominance and if she had daddy issues, I'd be happy to fill them. I knew her father wasn't in the picture and that her mom was a controlling bitch who wanted her out of the house. Hell, she wanted Mary on the other side of the country so she didn't interfere in her latest fling.

No wonder she wanted comfort from me. No wonder she wanted me to take her first. I wasn't letting some pimply-faced teenager touch her pure skin. If someone was going to defile her, it was going to be me. And I had. Fuck, she'd stood in the corner like a scolded little girl, showing me her ass with my pink handprint on it.

If she hadn't liked it, I wouldn't have done it, but her nipples had hardened even more, her cheeks had flushed and her pussy had practically dripped like a faucet as she obeyed me.

I was hard again, and I gripped the base of my dick. Needless to say, I woke up with a hard-on, and I'd jacked off in the shower. I finished quickly—it was easy, effortless almost. I just had to think about her, from those full breasts and ass to her thin waist and slender legs. She was every man's fantasy, and she was mine. I came again, amazed at how much cum was shooting from my balls. I had to stop, had to save it up for her. To load up that pussy and watch as it dripped out.

I messaged her early in the morning to come over at noon, not at her usual time so she could sleep in. I'd worked her hard last night. I would make lunch for the two of us. I told her I was working from home, so I could look after Ashley in the morning. I still needed to go to a meeting this afternoon and I was pleased to know she'd be here waiting for me when I got home. Would she be in just a slutty skirt and braless again? Shit, my dick dripped more pre-cum.

It took her a while to reply and tell me she'd be here by lunch time. Good. I wasn't going to wait much longer than that to get my hands on her. I knew I had a shit-eating grin on my face. She was not a virgin anymore. Because of *me*. That thought made me ecstatic. There was something so thrilling about having sex with a virgin. A sexy, naughty virgin named Mary.

It made me feel special, that out of all the people she could lose it with, she'd picked me. I knew boys and men were lining up to date and sleep with her. With a body and face like hers, it was just expected. And yet, she'd wanted me and I wasn't going to share her with anyone else. If a boy came sniffing around, he'd know who she belonged to. Who her pussy belonged to. I'd marked it well and good.

I couldn't wait to stare into her emerald eyes. I memorized them by now. I didn't care if I was being a sappy shit, but I could lose myself just staring at her. I knew exactly what was it about Mary that just drew me to her. It wasn't only her beauty, but who she was as a person.

She was independent, and never let anyone walk all over her, and yet, underneath such a strong, icy demeanor, I knew she was the most loving, understanding, and caring woman I'd ever had the pleasure to meet. And she had a submissive nature that just wanted to please me. To obey me. She always did what I asked, whether it was to bring Ashley to the park or to strip in front of me and play with herself. She did all I asked with no hesitation and questions. I had to wonder what else she'd do for me on command. No longer a virgin, I looked forward to doing all kinds of naughty things with her. She might be prim and proper outside of this house, but with me, she was a dirty, dirty girl.

I couldn't wait to see her, and with all the work I had to do, that came quickly. Before I knew it, I was racing down the stairs to open the door when the bell rang.

The moment I opened the door to welcome her in, I knew something wasn't right. I always looked forward to seeing her youthful smile or mischievous smirk. She knew how to use her sweetness and sexiness to her advantage and at the right time. My dick liked both and responded every time. Now though, there was neither, and I felt a sudden squeeze in my heart. Something was wrong, and I wanted to see her smile again.

"Are you alright, little girl?" I asked, resting a hand on her shoulder. I used that endearment with her to know I wanted her to answer me or she'd be over my knee.

"I'm fine," came her reply. I knew better than to let that go. I'd had enough ex-girlfriends to know that 'I'm fine' meant something was definitely wrong.

"You know you can tell me anything, right?" A sudden thought came to my head, one that actually had me nervous. "Is it about last night? Do you regret what happened?"

I almost breathed a huge sigh of relief when she automatically shook her head. Her eyes widened and her lips parted to shout, "No! Of course, not! I just—"

The heavens must have been siding with her because in that moment, Ashley began to cry, and Mary used that as an excuse to put an abrupt halt to our conversation and leave me to tend to her with a million more questions in my head. I wasn't going to let this go. She shouldn't be bottling up her problems all to herself. She had to know she could talk to me. I was going to make her see that, that there was more to this than just sex. We had all afternoon.

It was three hours later when Ashley finally went down for a nap and Mary and I could talk once again. I asked her to follow me into my office and I went to sit in my chair, and she made a move to sit on the leather one on the other side of my desk. I was quick to shake my head.

"Sit on my lap," I said, patting my thigh.

She froze for a second before walking over to me. With her legs dangling over my left thigh, she breathed out a comfortable sigh of relief while I wrapped a firm arm around her waist.

"Now tell me what's wrong…"

"You sound like a dad," was her immediate

response. "Although I don't really know how a dad's supposed to act like. Mine was absent." She was quick to correct herself. "Or at least, you act and sound how I think a dad's supposed to be like…"

"That's why you call me Daddy, isn't it?" I asked, my hand on the side of her waist while the other wrapped around her nape. I wanted her to look at me, not to hide anything. "I'm here to listen and help you and give you whatever you need, whether it's a good, hard fucking or a spanking over my knee."

She was trying to stop herself from crying, but I needed to let her know she had nothing to worry about. Crying was okay, especially if I got to hold her as she did it. Softly, I moved my hands from her waist and neck to wrap them around her entire torso tightly, pulled her into me so her head was tucked beneath my chin.

I started to play with her hair, to stroke it gently, and it was then she finally broke down. She told me how she and her mother fought earlier, told me how she didn't want to move across the country and that she wanted to stay in town and work at a pre-school. She told me how she could easily get a job here if she stayed, but her mother wanted anything but. By then end, she was all out of tears, and my arms were wrapped even tighter around her. I pulled my head away from hers before I began to kiss her on the lips, cheeks, and forehead. My arms remained around her, never letting go, and her hands had found their way

His Virgin Nanny

around my waist and up to my back. She hugged me as tight as she could, and it was the most comfortable feeling ever.

"Everything will be alright, Mary," I said. "I'm always here for you."

She nodded her head, closing and opening her lips from time to time. Finally, she said, "Will you help me apply to the local colleges? I already did some research, and there's one here that offers teaching certificates."

I beamed at her.

"Of course!" I shook my head and told her she didn't need to look so nervous asking me for help. I reminded her again that she could come to me for anything, and with that, I helped her off my lap and told her we were getting to work. "We'll start right now!"

She thought I was teasing her. I definitely wasn't, and I let her sit on a chair beside mine, gave her my laptop to work on. She started filling out the application, and after two hours of diligent effort on her part—I worked on my latest project beside her—the form was completed and submitted. I told her I'd help her research on the neighboring colleges as well, so at least she had a few to choose from.

"I'm relieved to know I have some options, that I might be able to stay in town," she said, putting the lid down on the laptop. Sitting back in the chair, she looked drained.

She needed a break and a naughty idea crossed my

mind. There was no second guessing though, and since I knew she would love it, I bent down, put my hands on her waist and lifted her off the chair and placed her ass down on my desk. I pushed the papers away, settled in my computer chair, and spread her legs wide. I heard her suck in a breath at the realization of what I was about to do before she took a fistful of my hair, squeezed, and let her head fall backward.

Eagerly and with a naughty smirk tainting my lips, I impatiently worked her panties off. She arched her back when my finger rubbed faintly against her clit and she let out a soft, feminine moan when I leaned down and with my tongue, teased her entrance. I wanted to take her slowly. To know there was more than one way for me to pleasure her. I wanted to savor eating her out, because, fuck, she tasted so good, and to give her the ultimate experience. I didn't want to rush doing this to her since it was her first time to have her pussy eaten. I wanted to hear her screams, feel when her fingers tangled in my hair, the breathy moans, the dripping arousal.

"Gabe…uh…" Her womanly voice filled the room, and I could feel my dick grow bigger and harder. It wanted in, now, but it wasn't in charge. At least not right now. Femininity really was the biggest turn-on. "That feels so good…"

I slipped a finger inside, found that little hook inside her pussy. It set Mary off like a firework. It felt so deep when it really wasn't, and it'd never failed to make a woman go crazy, and with the way Mary was moaning and thrusting her hips against my fingers, I knew she thought it was amazing as well. After a while, I wanted to add another layer to her experience, so I began to lick her pussy and mixed it with a little sucking and faint biting. At the same time, I moved my fingers much faster in and out of her, and I could feel her start to shake against me.

"I'm gonna come…Gabe…I'm gonna…"

"Let go, baby," I said. "Relax…let Daddy taste your juices."

And it was the sweetest taste I'd ever had, both figuratively and literally. She milked my finger while I licked up every drop of her desire. It was safe to say that it took her a while before she finally stood up from my desk. I couldn't keep the boyish grin off my face to see her so done in. Yeah, I could please the fuck out of my girl.

7

Mary

I rushed to get to Gabe's place, eager to share the good news. I couldn't *fucking* believe it. I squeezed the documents in my hand and got in my car as fast as I could. There was no one at home, my mom went out of town with her fiancé, so there was no one to reprimand me and tell me how bad a decision I was making. I knew *this* was the right decision and she was just being selfish. This wasn't about her. It was about me, what I wanted, what would make me happy.

I rang the doorbell, and in my excitement, it was only then I realized that I wasn't even sure if he was home. I wasn't supposed to come over today. It was my day off and I hadn't once stopped by on an off day.

Suddenly, I felt nervous. I honestly had no idea why. Gabe had been supportive all along, yet I felt foolish all of a sudden, driving over to his place on a whim. Would he want me here? *Where could he be?* My paranoid brain started to think. Yesterday, when we were together, he didn't mention his plans for today. He only mentioned that the worst of his workload had passed, so he was excited to enjoy the slower pace at the office. That meant we could spend time together, but why didn't he invite me to come over today? Was I only useful when I needed to look after Ashley? Did he only fuck me on my work days so that it was just a work-with-benefits thing? At that thought, I couldn't help the sudden sinking feeling in my heart. I was becoming paranoid and clingy, two things I knew were a turn-off.

I placed a finger on each of my temples and started to rub. I took deep breaths and told myself to not be a jealous bitch of whomever he was with. We weren't exclusive, but the idea of him telling some other woman to go stand in the corner had me ready to grab a hatchet. Did he play the Daddy role with someone else? We hadn't determined the status of our relationship yet, but *fuck it*, I didn't want to and wasn't going to admit it out loud, but I was starting to have feelings for him. *Very* deep ones. Ones that had me wanting to be his only little girl, to be the only one he licked and sucked, fucked and cared for.

Ughhh. I squeezed my eyes shut, and with perfect timing, the door opened, and I stared into familiar blue eyes as I did yesterday and the days before. My heart leapt at the sight of him.

"Mary...you're here," he said, shock tinging his face. "Are you alright?"

"Y-yes..." I stuttered a bit until I mustered the best smile I could. "I came over because..." I squeezed the documents in my hand, and he noticed. Slowly, he reached his arm out and took the papers away from me, looked through them. A smile slowly spread across his face.

"An acceptance letter to a teaching program *and* a job offer at a pre-school?" He grin was as wide as a Cheshire cat now, from ear to ear, but what took me by surprise the most was when he closed the distance between us and planted a full kiss on my mouth. "I'm so proud of you."

With those words, I melted into his arms, as he took me inside and kicked the front door closed behind us.

Gabe

"What time...is your mom...d-dropping off Ashley?" Mary asked me in between heavy breaths.

We spent the whole day watching movies, from romantic comedies and dramas to action and foreign language films. The only time we took a break from staring at my huge TV screen was when I called the nearby Chinese restaurant for delivery. I asked Mary if

His Virgin Nanny

she wanted to go out to celebrate her two victories – getting accepted into the college she wanted and nabbing a job – but she preferred to just stay in and cuddle.

It was so cute how she said it even – that she wanted to cuddle and have me for herself. It was a glimpse into a different side of her. She was usually so confident, both in the way she moved and acted, and seeing her being shy and unsure for a moment was a sight forever ingrained in my brain. That she showed it all to me made me feel, well, like a fucking rock star.

"Gabe…" she breathed out heavily.

Under the thick blankets, my fingers had found their way to her panties and were rubbing the lace material against her. I noticed how her breathing had turned ragged, and she wasn't watching the movie so much anymore. She closed her eyes for a moment as her head fell backward, and in a move of confidence, she wrapped her fingers around my wrist and moved my hand underneath her panties, showing me exactly where she wanted me to touch and how hard.

"Not tonight. Next week," I said, not stopping my finger play. "Enough about Ashley and my mother." They were the last two people I wanted to think about when I had my hand inside Mary's panties.

And with that, I flipped us over. Her back was splayed across the couch as I straddled her. My fingers continued to move and tease her pussy, and her hands roamed my back until they stopped at the end of my shirt to take it off. I did, with pleasure. I pulled the shirt over my head and threw it onto the floor before I began to remove her tank top. I couldn't help but smile widely at the sight of lace on her chest.

"You're wearing a bra," I said. "You never wear a bra." While I liked the easy access her going bare provided, the sexy lingerie had my dick throbbing.

She let out a light, feminine chuckle. *Ah...music to my ears.* "I didn't even think about changing. I rushed over here the moment I received those letters." The full confidence was back in her and she looked at me with the most mischievous of smiles. "You know why I never wear a bra."

"And why is that?" I asked, two fingers digging inside her, and she arched her back off the couch to push me in deeper.

"I was trying to get you to have sex with me."

"And I took your virginity."

"You've done more than that." The smirk on her face softened, and she made a move to pull her denim shorts and panties off. Clearly, this making out wasn't enough for my little vixen. "Y-you're...you care about me. You're not only constantly teaching me about sex, but with life in general. Gabe...you're the one who helped me apply to college and the jobs at the preschools. You've done more than anyone ever has... more than my own mother...you're like a boyfriend and father rolled into one. You take care of me and...I-"

She stopped there. Suddenly, she looked nervous,

but she hid it by closing her eyes and focusing on the way my fingers pushed in and out of her. I didn't want her to be nervous, never around me. She should already know by now that I'd always be here for her. But it seemed she didn't know that, that she'd said too much, or said something that was too serious too soon. Didn't she know she was The One for me? I wouldn't have fucked her otherwise.

"I think I like that," I said, getting her to look at me by hooking a finger under her chin. "Being your boyfriend and your Daddy."

Her eyes flew open at hearing those words and began to search mine. To look for the truth. Slowly, the nervousness and the wrinkle on her forehead began to disappear, but a little were still left, and so, I eased her nerves a bit. She was with me. She didn't need to be scared of anything.

I brought my face closer to hers and placed soft and hard kisses on her lips. Her hands moved to my clothes, pulling my shirt over my head and pushing my shorts off my legs until I was naked and my dick pressed against her thigh. She still had on her bra and panties though, but removing them was easy—and a joy.

"Gabe…" she breathed, when she felt me pushing my dick inside her. She arched her back off the couch again to give me better access. She wasn't a virgin any longer, her pussy opening for me nicely now. I'd had her so many different ways since that first time, but I had yet to come anywhere but nice and deep. I'd come in her mouth one of these days, but I just wasn't ready to give up fucking her.

I pushed and pushed until I couldn't go any deeper, the head of my dick bumping the end of her tight passage. I looked at her, saw the smile on her face, and couldn't help but kiss her again. There was just something about her – a lot of things actually. I couldn't pinpoint just one. She made me feel so much, and I never wanted those feelings to ever go away. She made life better, especially with her smiles, and of course, the steamy sex. With every hip thrust, with every one of her breathy cries, I thought, "Mine."

"Fuck…" I groaned, when she parted her legs wider so my dick could go even deeper. She rested the back of her ankles on my shoulder, her moans getting louder – almost screams – as I continued to thrust in and out of her. Fuck, how did she know to do that?

"So naughty," I murmured.

She grabbed at my hair, her breasts, my ass, and her clit, as I began to pick up my pace. She was screaming now, saying my name out loud for the neighbors to hear. I didn't care. I loved it when she shouted. It was like my trophy for winning her. It was definitely a stroke to my ego the way she lost herself in what I did to her, but more importantly, it told me she was more than enjoying every inch of my thick dick.

"Mary…" I breathed her name, and she knew what that meant. I felt my dick jerk inside her, and soon enough, my cum flooded her pussy. I continued to pump slowly, in and out, and when I finally pulled away, we both grinned at the sight of my cum dripping wet from her.

"Yeah, not a virgin any more. That pussy's mine." I met her green gaze. "Right, little girl?"

"Yes, Daddy. My pussy's just for you."

"Come here," I said to her, stretching my arm out, so she could rest her head on my chest. My couch was the right size, so that both of us could lie down squished against each other. She snuggled closer to me, our legs intertwined and with my arm splayed over her breasts. I planted a soft kiss on her hair.

"You know I'm not letting you go now, right?" I said. When she looked up at me, eyes full of surprise and love, she grinned.

"I'd like that because I don't want to go anywhere."

8

Mary

"Mary…"

I heard his voice. It was almost pleading, yet still commanding. He was my Daddy. I knew he wasn't my father. God, that was gross. But he was everything I wanted a man to be. He was emphatic, but dominating. I called him that blatantly now – Daddy – and every time, he responded positively. He'd either tell me to sit on his lap or snuggle into him, and I loved it. He felt so big and warm against my tiny frame. Every time I was with him, I felt like nothing bad was ever going to happen to me because he would protect me.

"Mary," he said again, walking over to where I was sitting on the couch. As he always did, he wound his arms around my waist and pulled me onto his lap. I dug my face in the crook of his neck and breathed out a sigh of relief. I automatically felt comfortable, like I could close my eyes and fall asleep. "What's bothering you? Come on, tell Daddy your problems. Didn't I tell you two nights ago that I wasn't letting you go?"

I nodded my head.

"See, then that means we have to be open with one another. There can't be any secrets between us if we want this to work out…you know," he continued, taking a pause and then, "Forever's a long time to be hiding stuff from one another."

He didn't need to prod me. With Gabe, I felt safe. Even better, I knew he was going to help me through my problems. That night he told me he was never letting me go, I heard and felt the sincerity in his words and actions. He wasn't just spouting off bullshit. He was a real man, he'd never do that. That night, for the entire time we were asleep, he held me tightly in his arms and against his chest.

With all these thoughts, I couldn't control my feelings anymore. The waterworks began, and they became worse when he hugged me even tighter and began stroking my hair.

"It's j-just…" *Fuck this*. I wasn't the prettiest when I was crying. I'd have bloodshot eyes, snot dripping from my nose, and some hair strands wet and sticky from the tears. But my feelings…I *fucking* couldn't control them any longer…it didn't help that Gabe held me with such love and care, as if he was prying the tears out of me. "This week's...j-just been so, *so* s-stressful...I-I had a huge fight with my mom." I wiped my nose with the back of my hand. "I-I don't want to stay...i-in t-that place anymore, so my friend, Sally, a-and I began looking...f-for apartments t-to move into."

"Shhh..." he said, still playing with my hair. He sat straighter on the couch, so I could rest my head on his chest, and I loved the feeling. When I told him I didn't want to get snot on his shirt, he told me to quiet down and that he didn't care. What was important to him was that I get my feelings out, so that I could feel better.

All I could think about was how lucky I was to have met him. He'd given me a job when I needed one and had taken on me at my sluttiest and most brazen, wanting to lose my virginity, but he'd given me so much more.

Here he was promising the world to me and taking on a huge responsibility. I knew I was a burden to him, but he treated me like he was the luckiest man in the world by having me. I felt like I was the lucky one too when he said, "Stop searching for apartments. I can help your friend, Sally, look for her own, but you're staying here with me."

My crying stopped for a moment as I tipped my head up to look at him. He was dead serious. *He wanted me to move in with him?* Wasn't that a huge step?

"Mary...I've told you again and again that you're

mine," he began, tipping his lips up into a smile. "When are you going to start believing me?"

It took a while for me to answer. I already knew what I was going to say. It was just…I couldn't believe this was happening. I'd been so bothered with looking for a new place, and here was Gabe solving my problem in less than a minute. The waterworks began again. I just couldn't help it. I couldn't believe he'd do this for me. I couldn't deny it now. He truly did care for me.

I responded to him by closing the distance between our lips. When he opened his mouth, I sucked in his breath before I darted my tongue out to play with his. His arms tightened around me, and my fingers began to play with his hair. He started to push me backwards to lie down on the couch when the doorbell rang. He ignored it, letting it ring, as we continued to make out, but when the sound came again, he pushed himself off me with the most irritated look on his face, like he was going to murder someone. I sat up from the couch and waited for him to come back.

Instead, I felt a cold shiver run up my spine at the familiar voice. Before I knew it, I was looking into the eyes of my mother.

9

abe

Fuck this.

I wasn't going to wait any longer. It'd been three days, and I still hadn't heard a thing from Mary. The night her mother came to my house, I saw the dynamic between the two, and I honestly had nothing good to say. From the way she moved and talked, I just couldn't respect Mary's mom. How such a beautiful, caring, and understanding person like Mary came from her womb I had no idea. They were just so different from each other, except for the green eyes maybe, but even those left room for discussion. Mary's eyes were a bright emerald, while her mother's were a murky green. I shook my head and cut my train of thought short. Hating Mary's mother wasn't going to do anything to help her. After waiting for three days and not a single phone call, I decided to take matters into my own hands.

I talked to Greg, who talked to Jane, who knew where Mary lived, and I was able to get her address. Why the fuck I hadn't known where she lived, I had no idea. Jane had been hesitant at first. She warned me that if I came unannounced while Mary's mother was there that she'd take it out on Mary. I asked Jane to be specific and explain what she'd just said. Did she beat her? I'd seen and touched every inch of Mary and hadn't seen one blemish or bruise. Verbal abuse? Jane said she didn't, just warned me not to do anything stupid. To ease her nerves, I told her to coordinate with Mary for her to sleep over when Mary's mother wasn't there. Then I'd go get my girl.

That was today.

And I was going to finally see her again.

It'd only been three fucking days, but it felt much longer. With her absence, I wanted her more and more. There was no warm body to hug me, no one to watch movies and cuddle with on the couch. No hot pussy, no pink nipples. No pert ass. I went home every night to an empty house since Ashley was still with my mother. I felt lonely in no time, and I wasn't going to hide it. I missed Mary.

I pulled my car into her driveway, and honestly, I

hadn't thought about what I was going to do or say yet. The only thing I'd planned was I that needed to make sure she was all right. I wanted to see her, kiss her, speak to her, and have sex with her in no particular order. Well, I wanted to do all of those things while I was having sex with her. I missed her and I was worried. I didn't like not being able to reach her and make sure she was taken care of. She called me Daddy and I took that seriously.

Taking care of her filled a need in me that I hadn't realized was missing. My niece, Ashley, was different. Yes, I took care of her, but being a little girl's uncle and being Mary's *Daddy* were two very, *very* different things.

My last serious girlfriend had never let me take care of her. She'd pushed and fought me every step of the way and I'd loved her enough to take a step back and only give her what she needed. Perhaps that was why it hadn't worked. I needed more. I needed to be in control and feel like I was making a difference in her life. But my ex hadn't wanted me hovering or interfering in her life or her decisions. I'd been on the sidelines and realized, after a few short months that I wasn't important to her other than as a sex toy. Someone to talk to. A buddy, not a man.

I'd put my needs second, only rediscovering them now, with someone new.

Mary.

She needed me. She let me take care of her. When I held her in my arms I felt invincible, like a real life superhero and I wasn't willing to give that up. Not when I knew she needed me as much as I needed her. Sure, there was a difference in our ages, but fuck that. She was mine. Mine to pamper and spank and make smile. Mine to hold on my lap and soothe. Mine to fuck until she was a sweaty, quivering mess.

Just…mine. And I wanted her back. I wanted her forever.

I got out of my car and walked toward the front door. I stretched my arm out to ring the bell, but before I could, the door swung open and Mary jumped into my arms. Skin against skin, I felt her cheek on the crook of my neck. It was slightly damp as she'd suddenly begun to cry when she saw me.

"Baby…" I said, stroking her hair. Her legs wrapped around my waist, and I carried her into her house. "Don't cry. I'm here now. Daddy's here."

"H-how…?" she stuttered. She'd quieted down with the crying but was still tearing up. "Y-you've never b-been…"

"Jane…I asked her to give me your address, and I made sure to come over when your mom isn't home. She's not here, is she?"

Mary shook her head quickly and buried her head again against my neck again. I felt her warm breath against my skin, and at the tingling sensation, I couldn't control my dick starting to get harder. She had that effect on me, and it probably didn't help that her breasts were squished against my chest.

"Let's go to my room," she said, and I made a move toward the staircase. Mary pointed to her bedroom. I placed her on the bed and she crawled backwards to rest against the headboard. I did the same and wrapped my arm around her shoulders and pulled her closer to me.

"You haven't been answering my calls and messages…Jane said your mother would confiscate your phone, but she'd let you have it for one hour each day…" At that, I couldn't help but tilt my lips downwards into a frown. I wanted to break something every time I called and messaged Mary and she didn't respond.

"W-what…?" I watched as Mary's eyes widened in shock. "I never received anything from you…" She looked away for a moment, in deep thought, before she met my eyes again. "Unless my mother erased everything. I wouldn't put it past her. She kept telling me how you were just using me. I'm young and inexperienced while you're so mature and worldly. My mom has been with a lot of guys, so I trusted her when it came to relationship advice…she told me successful guys like you never go for girls like me. That you probably fucked me for the fun of it and were going to move on. You go for successful, independent, badass women who know how to…"

His Virgin Nanny

She choked on the last and in that moment I really didn't like her mother very much for playing on Mary's insecurities like that.

My hands balled into fists, and I exhaled deeply to control my temper. Good thing her mother wasn't home or else I would've done something that could make Mary hate me.

"Bullshit," I said quickly. "You're perfect, Mary. You're smart and fun and beautiful. Your laugh makes me happy and you're kind. Caring."

She cried harder and when I asked what was wrong, she didn't answer me, but the blush on her cheeks did.

My innocent young woman needed another kind of reassurance. I buried my hand in her hair and lifted her lips to mine so I could talk against them. As I did so, I worked my hand down the front of her sweats, right under the hot, wet folds of her pussy lips so I could rub her clit. "You're perfect in bed. So hot," I dipped my fingers inside her hot core and rubbed her juices onto her clit. "So wet. You're always so wet for me. I love fucking you and your sweet, tight pussy." I rubbed harder and she lifted her hips off the bed, pressing into my hand as I kissed her neck and pushed her down on the bed. I was not going to fuck her in her room, not when her mother could come home any moment. But I was going to make sure she knew how I felt about her, how fucking beautiful and perfect she was.

I increased the speed of my hand and worked her body until she bucked beneath me, her orgasm rocking through her as she arched her neck back on a silent scream.

Just to prove my point, I didn't let her rest, but worked her with my fingers again, pushing two blunt tips deep inside to rub the base of her womb. She whimpered and I took her nipple into my mouth through her clothes, biting gently as my thumb worked her clit.

"Gabe! Daddy, please..." The breathless whisper made me shudder and I was so close, so damn close to blowing my cum all over the inside of my boxers that it took an epic force of will to hold back. My cum was for her, only for her. And I wanted it deep in her body so she'd know who she belonged to, who had claimed her. Who wanted her and no one else, ever.

"Come again for me, baby. Come all over my fingers."

That was all she needed, permission, an order from her Daddy, a safe place to be.

Her orgasm rolled through her and she'd never looked so beautiful, so fucking perfect as she did while she was losing it all over my fingers on her frilly pink bedspread.

When it was over, I pulled my hand from her and licked my fingers, holding her gaze as I did so she'd know I loved everything about her, including the hot taste of her cum on my hand. "No one has ever made me hotter than you do, baby."

I moved back up to the head of the bed and lifted

her into arms, hugging her tighter. She was my little stress ball. Wrapping my arms tightly around her did release some of the stress and anger I was feeling. "Your mother doesn't know me. You know me, Mary."

She nodded. "It's just, well... I'm...I don't have a lot of experience. And you're so much older and more experienced. You have a house and a job and a life and I'm nothing, you know. A worthless kid barely out of high school."

"That's your mother talking." Another point in the negative mother column. "You're sweet and kind and loving. You're beautiful, intelligent, fun. After everything I've told you, you still don't trust and believe me when I say I want to be with you?"

She shook her head at me once again. "I believe you…it's just…" A pause and then, "I know I shouldn't let my mother have power over me. I'm grown enough to be able to live my own life without her telling me what I should and shouldn't do."

I nodded my head, letting her continue.

"I'm sorry, Gabe. I let my mother get the best of me. That won't ever happen again."

"Shhh…" I said, taking her hand and intertwining our fingers together. "Don't apologize or you'll be in the corner again." Then, I hooked a finger under her chin to get her to look at me. I began to part my lips. It felt like the perfect time to say it, surrounded by her old life as I made the decision to offer her a new one.

"I love you, Mary. I really do."

Her smile was answer enough, but Mary always gave me far more than what I asked. "I love you, too. Daddy."

EPILOGUE

Mary

"IT'S GREAT TO FINALLY PUT A FACE TO THE NAME. I'VE heard so many great things about you!" Bethany began, standing proud in her military uniform. She hadn't been home long, and already I missed my days with Ashley. But now that I was in the teaching program and working at the pre-school, I had to admit that I didn't have time to watch Ashley much any more.

"And please, looking after my child when I specifically told my brother to do so? I love you forever!"

I couldn't help but burst out laughing. "Ashley is a little angel. We got along great, didn't we, squirt?" I spoke the last to the little girl playing on the floor. Gabe's sister was a character on her own, and with the way she spoke and acted, I could see the similarities she had with her brother. They both loved to banter, with no topic off limits, and it was all the more amusing when they were doing it to each other. Ten minutes in, and the two of them already managed to make me snort with laughter—quite unladylike. Which just made me laugh more.

By the time the party ended two hours later, tears streamed down my face and my cheeks actually ached from all the laughing.

"The only tears you'll be crying from now on are tears of joy, alright?" she said, as she came over to me after she'd managed to say "goodbye" to the friends and relatives she invited over. We were standing in the living room, the now empty space eerily empty with just family members here, like we were all in shocked silence. But Bethany smiled and gave me a quick hug. "I swear, if my brother hurts you, he'll be answering to me!"

"Wait, what?" Gabe exclaimed. "Shouldn't you be protecting me? I'm your brother."

We all shared a round of laughter at that before Ashley came running towards us, begging Bethany to pick her up. In one quick swoop, Ashley was in Bethany's arms and then on her shoulders. When I turned my head to find Gabe, he was down on one knee before me.

We were in the very center of the room with his family surrounding us in a loose circle. I turned to look at Bethany – this was supposed to be her 'Welcome Back' party, but she had a knowing smile on her face, a smile that made me begin to shake as I turned back to look down at the man I loved kneeling before me.

"Mary, I love you. You are the light in my life and you make me happier than I ever thought I could be. Will you marry me, baby?" he asked, and I could only stare at his face. He had his hand stretched out with a ring in a box, but I was too blinded by him and his proposal to even take a glance at the ring. I knew what my answer was going to be. We'd talked about this and started to plan our future together. This was the obvious next step but I'd never dreamed I'd get this. Gabe on one knee in front of the world asking me to be his.

Heat rushed to my face and I felt lightheaded, giddy with happiness as I tried to remember how to talk. My response came out jumbled and a little strained as I forced words past the lump in my throat.

"Yes! Yes, I'll marry you."

And with that, his family around us broke into applause as Gabe slid the ring onto my finger, stood up, and then pulled me away from everyone. The moment we were alone in his dining room with the sliding doors shut, he pushed me up against a wall and buried his nose in my hair, my neck, his hot, heavy breaths against my skin sending goose bumps all over me. I was instantly turned on, the muscles inside my pussy clenching and desperately wanting him inside me.

"You're going to be my wife."

I could only nod at that.

"You're going to have my baby."

I couldn't help but smile from ear to ear, then nod again.

"And we're going to start now."

I gasped when he lifted me up, pushed me against the wall, undid the front of his pants and filled me up with his hard dick. I'd been teasing him the whole day that I wasn't wearing any underwear and I was shocked and thrilled, so hot and wet his hard length slid inside me like we were made to be together.

"Yes, Daddy! Yes." I whispered the words I knew would make him hard and hot and out of control. I felt wild, and totally loved, and I wanted him to be just as wild, just as needy.

My eagerness for him, for letting him take control was one of the things he loved about me. I was up for anything, and he never failed to mention that. Being in a relationship with him was effortless, like how it was supposed to be. We never argued because we knew how to communicate. When we had problems, it was us against the problem instead of me against him. We were a partnership, an exciting one at that. We made each other's lives easier and more fun, and even though I was young, I knew this kind of love was rare.

"I'm going to come inside you…fill you up…" he said, thrusting in and out and starting to pick up the pace. "One day, you're going to carry my baby. We're going to create something so beautiful together…"

"I love you, Daddy," was all I could say. Never did I dream that I'd have the perfect relationship. I had seen many of my mother's failed ones and been desensitized to the idea that a perfect relationship actually existed, and here I was with one.

"I love you more," Gabe responded, and with that, he thrust harder and faster and began rubbing my clit. He pounded into me relentlessly, and my nails dug into his back and my teeth into his neck to stop myself from screaming. His family was barely a few feet away, and here we were, both about to go over the edge.

"I'm gonna come, Gabe…I'm gonna…"

"Together, baby," he said, pressing a hard kiss onto my mouth. "Together."

He caught my scream with his kiss, the taste of him on my lips heaven as his body jerked and pulsed inside me, my pussy milking him dry, making a claim of its own.

I might be his, but he was also mine, and with his dick balls deep inside me, his body trembling and shaking, his ring on my finger, every doubt fled, years of insecurity and wondering flew out the window and I was home. Really, really home in Gabe's arms. My Daddy.

I went into this wanting to lose my virginity. Never did I dream that I'd get my "happily ever after."

DID YOU MISS THE FIRST BOOK IN THIS SERIES? READ ON for a sneak peek of Chapter One of Jane's story...

WANT MORE? READ HIS DIRTY VIRGIN

He might be the bad boy, but she's the one who's dirty.

HIS DIRTY VIRGIN - CHAPTER 1

ecca

I FELT THE BLOWOUT MORE THAN HEARD IT. I EXPECTED a flat tire to have a huge boom or pop, but no. The wheel began to shake and my steering became erratic. Thankfully, I wasn't going too fast and the road was straight. I was able to pull off to the side without sliding into the ditch. I sat there, heart racing, adrenaline pumping, cars whizzing by.

I wanted to scream my lungs out. A flat! I didn't need this. I had more than enough on my plate already. I'd just come from lunch with my father, and as usual, it ended up with him telling me how much of a disappointment I was and me walking out of the restaurant. All I'd done was tell him I was taking up pre-med for my major, not that I decided not to go to college to be a carnie with the circus. No matter how uncomfortable the lunch, and his blatant disapproval, I still wasn't – and *never* would – go into business.

"Others would die to be in your position!" he'd told me at the restaurant. "While your classmates are scurrying to find an entry-level job or even an unpaid internship in the hopes they can land full-time offers four years from now when college is over, I'll put you in the fast track. You can be a manager next month. Why don't you want that?"

"I just graduated high school!" I'd responded, raising my voice. He'd been listening but hadn't heard me. He never had. "Can't I just have fun for a while?"

The expression on his face had morphed. The wrinkles on his forehead deepened, and every muscle on his body stiffened. The look wasn't new. I'd seen it countless times – sadness, disappointment, and hopelessness all mixed together – but it still always bothered me, as if I could never do right by him.

"Life isn't about 'having fun'. You'd know that if I didn't hand everything to you on a gold, diamond-encrusted platter. You never had to work a day in your life, Becca. Of course, all you want to do is 'have fun'. That's on me…to have given you everything. I feel like I've failed as a father."

Everything he'd given me came at a price and that

was going into the family business. If I joined him, he'd think it all had been worth it. If I didn't do it, then I was a slacker. A slacker who wanted to be a doctor, but still, to him, a freeloader. Spoiled. I couldn't have sat there a minute longer, so I walked out of the restaurant.

My dad had always put himself up on a pedestal. It was infuriating. But there was still that little voice in my head, that little voice telling me that I should listen to him, that he just loved me too much and wanted what was best for me. He loved me enough to want me to take over his empire someday. And that was why he'd given me everything I needed and wanted.

There was no denying he and my mom always gave me the best. They sent me to the best private school, they gave me all the gadgets and tools I'd needed and wanted to make studying easier, they hired the best coaches and personal trainers so that I'd become a state-level athlete. Even without my father paying my tuition, I'd had multiple academic and sports scholarships to choose from. Even after my mother died eight years ago and my father remarried, the help didn't stop. Anything I asked for, I got.

Yeah...maybe he failed as a father because he spoiled me too much, but I hadn't wasted any of it. I'd excelled at it all. I was going to be a damn doctor.

"Fuck." The profanity left my mouth when I realized I'd been sitting in my car for too long, and I was starting to sweat.

It was June, the middle of the day with the summer sun was beating down, and here I was with a flat tire. I had a spare in the trunk, but I was definitely not in the mood to change it. I had no choice. Tires didn't change themselves.

I swung open the driver's door and shut it with a bang before I went to the trunk and unlocked it. With all the strength I could muster, I did my best to pull the tire out and rolled it as close as I could to the flat. I walked back to the trunk to look for the wrench. I could feel the sun burning my back, the sweat dripping down my face and arms. I wanted to be anywhere but here, do anything but this, except maybe go back to the restaurant with my dad. As I kept complaining in my head, I loosened up the nuts. They were on so tight, I wasn't sure if I could get them all.

"You need help?"

That voice. All male, deep and rumbly.

I dropped the tool with a clang and stood, tipped my head up, my eyes moving from muscled arms covered in tattoos to a sun-kissed angular jaw, and finally, striking pale blue eyes. I instantly stilled, my heart hammering once again. He was easily one of the most attractive men I'd ever seen, if not the most. And he had tattoos! They were a dangerous—but oh-so sexy —touch I never knew could be so hot.

"Y-yes, please," I managed to croak out.

He moved to glance down at the tire, then at me. "I'm Jake Huntington." He easily introduced himself, sticking his big hand out for me to shake. "Just so you can report my name to the police when I get in your car and drive off." My eyes instantly went wide, and he took notice. A wicked grin spread across his face. "Just kidding. I can't drive away with a flat tire." His eyes raked up and down my figure, from my mop of brown hair and all the way down to my wedge sandals.

"Seriously, it was a joke. Ever heard of one?"

I realized I was still staring, not responding. I shook my head. "I'm sorry, but this flat hasn't put me in a joking mood. This day's just getting worse, and it's barely after lunch."

"You and me both," he grumbled.

"I'm Becca, by the way. Becca Madison." I noticed the look on his face—recognition. It was the same expression I had just moments ago when he introduced himself.

Jake Huntington...the name definitely rang a bell. He looked like the same Jake I'd met back at my mother's funeral dinner years ago. The same eye and hair color. Only now, the teenager I once knew had grown into a man. Crazy for me to remember after so long, but he was...unforgettable. The Jake beside me now was *all* man. He was much taller, more muscular, and stood proud like he had his shit together. Maybe he did, even if he left home and turned his back on his family. Yeah, I'd heard the story because Jake's dad was my father's corporate attorney.

It had been big news in our small town—when Jake ran away. Well, he hadn't *run* away like a five-year-old. He'd been studying pre-law when he decided he didn't want to become a lawyer and his father had flipped. I didn't know the details of what happened after that, but I hadn't heard a peep about Jake since. All I knew was that he wasn't considered part of the family anymore.

"Whatever happened to law school?"

A slow smile spread across his face. "I'm infamous enough that a pretty girl on the side of the road knows who I am."

I shrugged. "You know who I am by my name, just as I know you."

He slowly shook his head. "You don't know me. Just what you've heard."

I looked him over from his boots to his very well-worn jeans to his black t-shirt which left nothing to the imagination. "You're right. So what happened to law school?"

A smirk made its way onto his face at my repeated question. *Damn*, he was hot. "Nothing. I decided not to go and instead started my own business after I got my degree."

"Oh? What business?" I guessed his life was turning out much better than mine ever would. I didn't think I could do what he did, turn my back on my family and make it on my own. Telling my father off at lunch was one thing, but go solo? I had no idea how I'd make it. Maybe my father was right. He'd given me everything, and I didn't know how to stand on my own two feet.

He stuck his elbow out. "Does my arm say enough?" I couldn't miss the corded forearms, the bulging biceps. *A gym?* "Tattoo parlor."

I nodded my head. "Was it your mother that steered you in that direction?"

He looked shocked at my question until a smile surfaced once again on his face. "You remember my mother?"

"Of course." I smiled back. "I might be younger than you, but our families are pretty close. Your mom, she's…definitely a character."

His mother was the antithesis of what our fathers were like. They were masters of the universe. At least of this town. They were powerful and rich. They were the type of people that no one could say no to, even if their demands seemed unrealistic. People under them just had to make things happen.

"Definitely." At that, we both shared a laugh. "But yeah, she nurtured my interest in the arts, taught me how to enjoy life and not take it so seriously. Because of that, I started drawing when I needed to de-stress. She'd bring me along when she went out with some friends sometimes. I knew I'd get bored sooner or later, so I'd always bring my sketchpad, and when they saw my art, all of them were asking me if I could tattoo my artwork."

"Oh, wow…so your business started organically."

We stood on the side of the road chatting until he suddenly remembered the tire. He grabbed the tire iron and knelt by the flat, got to work.

He seemed like a nice guy and he'd gotten out from under his father's wrath. I envied him that.

"Yeah, they'd see my art, but there was always a deeper meaning whenever they chose their designs, and that—the stories and meanings behind the tattoos—turned my hobby into a passion. People sharing their experiences through art is such a great way to connect. It's as if once they see you have a tattoo, their walls instantly come down. Even if they're doing it as a dare or out of drunkenness, they're still showing some kind of vulnerability—they're giving me and everyone else the opportunity to judge, and that's the thing—I never judge. I embrace." I was too engrossed listening to him I hadn't realized he was finished with replacing my tire. "There you go, princess."

I raised my eyebrow up at him. *Princess?* I followed his eyes and watched as they lingered for a moment on the pearls on my ears and around my neck and then my pale pink sundress. *Oh.*

"Stop by sometime." He reached in his back pocket and took a card out from his wallet. "The shop. I saw the look on your face earlier. You're curious. Come check it out for yourself."

"Sure," I responded, meeting his eyes. I mustered up the courage to smile at him. *God*. I could stare at him all day. I was curious. Not as much about a tattoo as about him, and exactly what it would feel like to have a certified bad boy kissed me. "I will. I'll stop by."

Get His Dirty Virgin now!

GET A FREE BOOK!

Join my mailing list to be the first to know of new releases, free books, special prices and other author giveaways.

http://freehotcontemporary.com

ALSO BY JESSA JAMES

Bad Boy Billionaires

Lip Service

Rock Me

Lumberjacked

Baby Daddy

The Virgin Pact

The Teacher and the Virgin

His Virgin Nanny

His Dirty Virgin

Club V

Unravel

Undone

Uncover

Beg Me

Valentine Ever After

ABOUT THE AUTHOR

Jessa James grew up on the East Coast but always suffered a severe case of wanderlust. She's lived in six states, had a variety of jobs and always comes back to her first true love – writing. Jessa works full time as a writer, eats too much dark chocolate, has an iced-coffee and Cheetos addiction, and can't get enough of sexy alpha males who know exactly what they want – and aren't afraid to say it. Dominant, alpha-male insta-luv is her favorite to read (and write).

Sign up HERE for Jessa's Newsletter:

http://jessajamesauthor.com/mailing-list/

www.ingramcontent.com/pod-product-compliance
Lightning Source LLC
LaVergne TN
LVHW011847060526
838200LV00054B/4206